RACIAL VIOLENCE
Tearing at the Fabric of American Life

by Sue Bradford Edwards

© 2024 ReferencePoint Press, Inc.
Printed in the United States

For more information, contact:
ReferencePoint Press, Inc.
PO Box 27779
San Diego, CA 92198
www.ReferencePointPress.com

ALL RIGHTS RESERVED.

No part of this work covered by the copyright hereon may be reproduced or used in any form or by any means—graphic, electronic, or mechanical, including photocopying, recording, taping, web distribution, or information storage retrieval systems—without the written permission of the publisher.

Content Consultant: Jeffrey S. Adler, PhD, Professor of History, University of Florida

---

LIBRARY OF CONGRESS CATALOGING-IN-PUBLICATION DATA

Name: Bradford Edwards, Sue, author.
Title: Racial violence: tearing at the fabric of American life / by Sue Bradford Edwards.
Description: San Diego, CA: ReferencePoint Press, Inc., 2024 | Audience: Grade 9 to 12 | Includes bibliographical references and index.
Identifiers: ISBN: 9781678205829 (hardcover) | ISBN: 9781678205836 (eBook)
The complete Library of Congress record is available at www.loc.gov.

CONTENTS

VISUAL CHRONOLOGY	4
INTRODUCTION	6
THE SHOOTING OF STEPHON CLARK	
CHAPTER ONE	10
A BLOODY HISTORY	
CHAPTER TWO	22
SHOOTINGS OF BLACK PEOPLE	
CHAPTER THREE	34
VIOLENCE AGAINST NATIVE WOMEN	
CHAPTER FOUR	46
ANTI-ASIAN VIOLENCE	
Source Notes	58
For Further Research	60
Index	62
Image Credits	64
About the Author	64

Visual Chronology

1830 — President Andrew Jackson signs the Indian Removal Act.

1831 — Nat Turner's slave revolt takes place.

1851 — Congress passes the Indian Appropriations Act.

1865 — Slavery in the United States is abolished with the Thirteenth Amendment.

1882 — Congress passes the Chinese Exclusion Act.

1918 — The Porvenir Massacre takes place in Texas.

1919 — A race riot occurs in Chicago, Illinois, after a white man stones and drowns a Black man.

1921 — The Tulsa Race Massacre takes place.

1942 — President Franklin D. Roosevelt signs an executive order that forces Japanese Americans into incarceration camps.

2010 — Sumi Gail Juan, a Native American woman, goes missing.

2012 —  George Zimmerman shoots and kills Trayvon Martin in Sanford, Florida.

2014 — Police shoot and kill Michael Brown in Ferguson, Missouri.

2018 —  Stephon Clark is killed by police in Sacramento, California.

2019 —  Kiana Klomp goes missing, but her story is ignored by the media; President Donald Trump creates the Task Force on Missing and Murdered American Indian and Alaska Natives.

2020 — Police officer Derek Chauvin kills George Floyd; anti-Asian hate crimes begin to rise during the COVID-19 pandemic.

2021 —  Denny Kim is attacked for being an Asian American; the Missing and Murdered Unit is created to help find murdered and missing Native people; the COVID-19 Hate Crimes Act becomes law.

INTRODUCTION

The Shooting of Stephon Clark

It was 9:13 p.m. on March 18, 2018, when police officers responded to a 911 call in Sacramento, California. The caller said a Black man in a dark hoodie and pants had been breaking car windows and was hiding in a backyard. Officers found three damaged vehicles. Deputies in a police helicopter also saw the suspect break a sliding glass door and jump a fence into a backyard. They directed officers Terrence Mercadal and Jared Robinet to the suspect.

Mercadal later reported that he and Robinet rounded a corner and saw the suspect pointing a gun at them. He said that in the beam of his tactical light he saw either a metallic reflection or a muzzle flash.

Mercadal and Robinet fired twenty times. They hit the suspect, Stephon Clark, with seven shots, including six in the back. The police report said they were joined by additional officers. Clark didn't move as the officers discussed needing shields to approach him. A thorough search yielded only Clark's cell phone and no firearm. Officers then cuffed him and began first aid. An autopsy later revealed that it took Clark between three and ten minutes to die. During this time, officers were searching for a gun.

Clark had been shot in his grandmother's backyard. Police officers knocked on her door and asked if the man they shot had tried to get inside. She told them the only person who would try to enter would be her grandson coming home.

After Stephon Clark was shot and killed, protesters gathered in Sacramento City Hall to demand accountability. They wanted the officers charged.

Only then did she realize that they had killed her grandson in her backyard.

The Sacramento Police Department's investigation cleared the two officers of wrongdoing because Clark had fled from them, and the officers said they saw him take a shooting stance as if to fire on them. The investigation focused on the officers' belief that Clark was armed. District Attorney Anne Marie Schubert also questioned Clark's character. She presented information unrelated to the shooting that made him look bad. She said that in the days before his death, the mother of Clark's children had reported him to the police for abusing her. Schubert added:

> *We look at all these facts and circumstances, we look at everything. We have one question to answer. And that question is was there a crime committed? . . . There's no question that a human being died, but when we follow the law and our ethical responsibility, we will not be charging these officers with criminal liability for the death of Stephon Clark.*[1]

Clark's family said Schubert had conducted a smear campaign. "I don't care if he was a criminal. None of that matters," said Clark's mother, Sequette Clark. "What matters is how those officers came with lethal force around a corner, on a vandalism call, after my son and gunned him down—when he had nothing but a cellphone in his hand."[2]

Sacramento mayor Darrell Steinberg spoke to the press and apologized to the family for what had happened. Then he continued with a message to the larger community. "Today, the district attorney said she focused on a single question: Did the officers who shot Stephon Clark commit a crime? Her answer was, 'No,'" Steinberg said. "Our community and its leadership have different questions. Was the outcome wrong? Was the outcome unacceptable? The answer to both questions is yes."[3]

> "Today, the district attorney said she focused on a single question: Did the officers who shot Stephon Clark commit a crime? Her answer was, 'No.' Our community and its leadership have different questions. Was the outcome wrong? Was the outcome unacceptable? The answer to both questions is yes."
> —Sacramento mayor Darrell Steinberg

Religious leaders gathered outside Sacramento's City Hall to show their disapproval with Schubert's decision not to press charges. They were also upset that Schubert had attacked Clark's character. "This was a modern-day lynching in the city of Sacramento and the district attorney should be recalled for these shameful actions," said Pastor Kevin Kitrell Ross of Unity of Sacramento Church.[4]

National Public Radio examined the shooting deaths of unarmed Black people in the United States. It found that between 2015 and 2021 at least 135 unarmed Black people were killed by law enforcement. Clark's shooting was not an isolated incident. Every year, approximately 1,000 people are killed by police. Of these, 40 to 50 percent are minorities.

Racial Violence

Racial violence in the United States takes many forms. Hate crimes are one example. These are crimes committed against people because of their race or ethnicity, gender, nationality, religion, sexual orientation, or disability status. These crimes can include assaulting or injuring someone and touching him or her inappropriately. Damaging property with racist messaging is another example of a hate crime. Threatening to inflict physical damage to a person's body, family, or property is also considered a hate crime.

In addition, racial violence occurs when society acts against a group of people. One example is violence against unarmed Black people by law enforcement. Researchers and scientists study how racial violence impacts people's lives and what can be done about it. They work to educate people about racial violence. Despite these efforts, the number of crimes based on race increased between 2019 and 2020. As counted by the US Department of Justice, single-incident hate crimes rose from 3,963 in 2019 to 5,227 in 2020. To understand racial violence in modern society, one must first look at its history in the United States.

CHAPTER ONE

A Bloody History

Many different groups of people have been victims of racial violence in the United States, both historically and in the modern day. Native Americans have a long history of experiencing violence at the hands of the US government. In the 1800s, white settlers continued pushing Native American peoples off their traditional lands—something that had been happening for decades. The US Army sought to crush any Native resistance. In 1830, President Andrew Jackson signed the Indian Removal Act. This ultimately forced Native peoples

The US government forced Native Americans off their lands. Many Native people died from exhaustion, disease, malnutrition, and exposure on the Trail of Tears.

Starting in the 1830s, the US government moved Native Americans onto reservations. In 2022, many Native Americans on reservations lived in poverty.

in the East to give up their lands and move to the west side of the Mississippi River.

With the passage of the Indian Removal Act, the US government forced 100,000 Cherokee, Seminole, Choctaw, Chickasaw, and Creek peoples from their lands. Their removal opened up areas in Alabama, Florida, Georgia, Mississippi, Kentucky, and North Carolina for white settlement. During a journey of more than 1,000 miles (1,600 km), known as the Trail of Tears, 15,000 Native Americans died.

Competition for land continued as settlers pushed west past the Mississippi River. They came into conflict with both Native Americans who had been forcibly moved and the original Plains peoples, such as the Sioux. To subdue Native people and clear the land, Congress passed the Indian Appropriations Act of 1851. The act created land reservations where various Native American nations would live, opening the majority of their original territory for settlers. Native people were expected to remain on these reservations and feed their families by farming—even if they did not know how to farm or want to do it.

When Native Americans could not feed their families, they tried returning to their traditional ways of life. Multiple wars were fought between the US Army and Native peoples. The Apache Wars (1861–1886) took place in Arizona and New Mexico. The Sioux Wars (1851–1890) spread across fifteen states. Warfare periodically ended with the signing of a treaty and Native Americans giving up more land. The US Army did not limit itself to combating armed Native American warriors. In 1890, the Seventh Cavalry Regiment attacked a Lakota encampment near the Pine Ridge Reservation in South Dakota, killing between 250 and 300 people. Almost half of the people killed were children and

The Social Construct of Race

In the early 1900s, sociologist W. E. B. Du Bois was concerned that people discussed race as if it were something rooted in biology. Du Bois understood that it was a social construct, an idea invented by society. Scientists today agree with Du Bois. Svante Pääbo is a biologist and the director of the Max Planck Institute for Evolutionary Anthropology in Germany. He has studied the human genome, the full set of genetic material that makes people who they are. "What the study of complete genomes from different parts of the world has shown is that even between Africa and Europe, for example, there is not a single absolute genetic difference, meaning no single variant where all Africans have one variant and all Europeans another one, even when recent migration is disregarded," Pääbo said.

Humans are much more alike than they are different, with the same genetic variations found to differing degrees across continents and regions. To prove the point, the complete genomes of three scientists were compared. Two were of European descent and one was Korean. The two European scientists had more in common with the Korean scientist than they had with each other.

Megan Gannon, "Race Is a Social Construct, Scientists Argue," Scientific American, *February 5, 2016. www.scientificamerican.com.*

women, and others were unarmed men. This became known as the Wounded Knee Massacre.

In an attempt to destroy Native American cultures, the US government took Native children and put them in boarding schools. These schools operated from 1819 to the 1970s. Students had to cut their hair, speak only English, and learn farming and other trades. The schools were brutal places where children were physically, sexually, and emotionally abused. The children lost their languages, cultures, and traditional ways of life. At least 500 children died in these schools.

Violence Toward Black People

Racial violence against Black people in North America began when they were forced to come to the Americas as part of the slave trade. The transatlantic slave trade started in 1526 and lasted until the 1800s. During that time, 12.5 million men, women, and children were taken from Africa. Children made up approximately 26 percent of the captives. Government regulations limited how much weight a slave ship could carry. Since smaller captives weighed less, taking children let slavers force more captives onto each ship. Approximately 12 percent of enslaved people died during the journey from Africa to the Americas.

Half of all enslaved children died from malnutrition before they were one year old. Adults suffered from illnesses caused by malnutrition. These included kwashiorkor, a condition resulting from insufficient protein, and rickets, which is caused by a lack of vitamin D. White plantation owners who enslaved Africans often forced them to do grueling labor in the fields. Enslaved people could be punished at any time and were whipped, tortured, mutilated, and imprisoned.

Enslaved people struggled to regain their freedom. Some ran away from their captors. Others took part in slave revolts. One of the most famous revolts took place in 1831. Nat Turner was a slave in Virginia who planned to seize weapons and free as many enslaved people as he could. Turner began the revolt by killing his enslaver. Then he and a group of other Black people made their way to the town of Jerusalem, where weapons were located.

Almost 180,000 Black men joined the Union Army during the American Civil War. However, they still faced racial discrimination.

Within two days and nights, approximately sixty white people were killed. Turner's resistance was soon crushed by Virginia's militia and other armed white people. Rebellions were harshly put down. Trials were quick, and they were followed by hangings.

Some runaway slaves journeyed north using the informal network of assistance known as the Underground Railroad. Stations existed wherever a helper was willing to take a risk to hide runaways or move them toward freedom. Slave catchers were a constant threat.

The American Civil War (1861–1865) was waged between the South, also called the Confederacy, and the North, also called the Union. The South wanted to continue the practice of slavery, and it tried to break away from the United States to do so. Throughout the fighting, thousands of enslaved people fled north. Unprepared to deal with this influx, the federal government settled people into refugee camps where starvation and disease killed many. The Thirteenth Amendment passed in January 1865, abolishing slavery. The North won the Civil War that spring.

Racial violence toward Black Americans did not stop with the end of slavery. White resistance to their freedom included violence from groups like the Ku Klux Klan (KKK). The KKK tried to punish formerly enslaved people, known as freedmen, and their supporters through whippings and beatings.

Both members of law enforcement and the public took part in lynchings. This is when a mob murders a person. Victims were often hung. Some were set on fire, tortured, or decapitated. One infamous case took place in 1955 when fourteen-year-old Emmett Till was murdered in Mississippi after being accused of flirting with a white woman. No one was ever convicted of his murder. The National Association for the Advancement of Colored People notes that at least 4,743 lynchings occurred between 1882 and 1968.

Starting in the early 1900s, Black people began moving to the North, Midwest, and West to find jobs in factories. They also hoped to escape the racial violence they faced in the South, but racism has no geographical boundaries. East Saint Louis, Illinois, attracted 10,000 to 12,000 Black people between 1916 and 1917. On July 1, 1917, a rumor said a Black person had killed a white man, and rioters moved around East Saint Louis, conducting drive-by shootings, beating Black people, and setting fires. Some 6,000 Black people fled the area. Estimates of the dead vary from thirty-nine to 200 Black people killed.

Another riot took place in Chicago, Illinois. On July 27, 1919, a young Black man swimming in Lake Michigan drifted into a white-only area. A white man stoned and drowned him. Police refused to arrest anyone, even though Black witnesses had seen who was responsible. Angry crowds gathered on the beach and fighting broke out. The riot lasted for thirteen days and ended with twenty-three Black people and fifteen white people killed. The property damage left 1,000 Black families homeless.

Perhaps the best-known race riot is the Tulsa Race Massacre, which took place on May 31, 1921. Greenwood was a Black community in Tulsa, Oklahoma. It had its own stores, theaters, restaurants, hotels, and homes. When a nineteen-year-old Black man was accused of assaulting a white woman, anger erupted. It is estimated that 300 Black people were killed as whites moved through the community with rifles and machine guns, even dropping bombs from private planes. Greenwood burned to the ground.

Racism Against Hispanic People

In 1845, President John Tyler annexed the Republic of Texas, making this former Mexican territory a part of the United States. The next president, James Polk, wanted to expand US territory further. One area he set his sights on was land south of Texas known as the Nueces Strip. It lay between the Nueces River to the north and the Rio Grande to the south. Mexico said Texas's southern border was the Nueces River. But the United States said the border was further south, at the Rio Grande.

Polk ordered US Army troops into this disputed territory. When the Mexican military fired on them, killing eleven Americans, the US government declared war. Throughout the Mexican-American War (1846–1848), anti-Mexican bigotry led US soldiers to commit crimes against defeated Mexican soldiers and civilians. US soldiers raped, looted, and assaulted people—acts that would be considered war crimes today. The Treaty of Guadalupe Hidalgo ended the war. The United States gained control over the territories of modern California, Nevada, and Utah, along with parts of what are now Arizona, New Mexico, Oklahoma, Colorado, and Wyoming. Mexico also agreed to no longer contest Texas or the Nueces Strip. Suddenly, former citizens of Mexico were living in US territory.

US Border Patrol agents monitor the US–Mexico border to decrease illegal immigration. In 2021, some of these agents used unnecessary force and inappropriate language when encountering people seeking refuge in the United States, sparking outrage and an investigation.

Many white Texans held racist views against Mexicans. This led to violence against Mexicans in the United States, and racism against them continues today. One notable case was the lynching of Antonio Rodriguez in Rocksprings, Texas, in November 1910. Twenty-year-old Rodriguez had allegedly confessed to the murder of a rancher's wife. A mob took him from the jail, beat him, and burned him alive. Rodriguez was not the only suspect in the killing. Some people today still believe the rancher himself was guilty.

Another racially motivated murder occurred in September 1915. Jesus Bazan and his son-in-law Antonio Longoria had reported the theft of horses from their ranch to the Texas

Rangers, a law enforcement group. The Rangers decided that the pair of ranchers must be thieves and followed them, shooting them in the backs and leaving their bodies to rot.

Yet another case took place in 1918 with the Porvenir Massacre. On the morning of January 28, a group of Texas Rangers, local ranchers, and US soldiers seized fifteen men and boys of Mexican descent from the town of Porvenir, Texas. There was no trial before the fifteen people were executed. Many of their families abandoned their homes, farms, and ranches to seek shelter in Mexico, so the Mexican government investigated the killings. The Texas Rangers and ranchers submitted reports in an attempt to justify their actions, accusing the deceased of raiding a ranch one month earlier. In these reports, they claimed that they had been fired upon and had returned fire, killing the men and boys. The US State Department found no evidence of a shootout and confirmed that the men and boys had died while in Ranger custody. Texas

Zero Tolerance

In 2018, the US government began a zero-tolerance policy at the border with Mexico. Its goal was to deter people from illegally entering the United States. When families reached the border, US officials separated parents and their children. Writer Jaclyn Diaz explained, "Under the policy, adults who entered the U.S. from the southern border were prosecuted for illegal entry. Children can't be imprisoned with parents and other family members, so young kids were taken into federal custody—resulting in more than 3,000 children being separated from their families."

Nazario Jacinto-Carrillo, a Guatemalan, illegally crossed the border with his daughter into San Diego, California. When agents seized them, Nazario was told that if he returned to Guatemala his daughter would follow in two weeks. It took nearly three months, a team of lawyers, and media attention for them to be reunited. The zero-tolerance policy ended in 2021.

Jaclyn Diaz, "Justice Department Rescinds Trump's 'Zero Tolerance' Immigration Policy," NPR, *January 27, 2021. www.npr.org.*

governor William Pettus Hobby disbanded the group of Rangers, firing some of them and transferring others. This was a rare case in which the killers of Mexican Americans were punished.

The US Border Patrol was founded in 1924 to guard both the northern border with Canada and the southern border with Mexico. Officers were often recruited from racist groups like the KKK. In the 1930s, the organization's focus shifted to the Mexican border. Reports surfaced about agents using racist slurs and sexual comments even during stops within the United States, away from the border. Violence against Mexicans and Mexican Americans continued into the 2020s.

Anti-Asian Hostilities

Chinese immigrants first journeyed to the United States in large numbers in the 1850s. These immigrants aimed to find jobs, earn money, and send this money home to their families. They were willing to work for very low wages. They got jobs in mining, agriculture, textile factories, and railroad construction. By the early 1850s, approximately 25,000 Chinese workers had arrived. They made up roughly 10 percent of California's population.

Some white Californians believed that the Chinese brought disease. Others thought they were immoral drug users. And there were those who simply wanted to prevent people of color from affecting the predominantly white racial makeup of the country.

Chinese miners working in the California gold fields had to pay a foreign miners tax. White miners regularly tried to drive Chinese miners away. Even if police arrested the white attackers, California law blocked Chinese immigrants from testifying against them in court.

Coolie was the racist slang word for a Chinese worker, and some white people formed so-called anti-coolie clubs. In 1867, a white mob drove Chinese laborers from a San Francisco, California, building site. One Chinese worker was killed and twelve were injured. The Anti-Coolie Association came to the defense of the attackers, and they were released without getting charged.

The US government responded to the anti-Chinese sentiment, passing the Page Act of 1875 and the Chinese Exclusion Act of 1882. The Page Act prevented the immigration of Chinese women, who many believed would become prostitutes. It also blocked immigration of anyone with a felony conviction in China. The Chinese Exclusion Act greatly limited immigrants from China and prevented them from getting US citizenship. Erika Lee is a professor at the University of Minnesota. She says, "Beginning in 1882, the United States stopped being a nation of immigrants that welcomed foreigners without restrictions, borders or gates. Instead, it became a . . . gatekeeping nation. In the process, the very definition of what it meant to be an 'American' became even more exclusionary."[5] The Chinese Exclusion Act was repealed in 1943.

> "Beginning in 1882, the United States stopped being a nation of immigrants that welcomed foreigners without restrictions, borders or gates. Instead, it became a . . . gatekeeping nation. In the process, the very definition of what it meant to be an 'American' became even more exclusionary."
> —Professor Erika Lee, University of Minnesota

On December 7, 1941, Japan attacked the US naval base at Pearl Harbor, Hawaii. Afterward, anti-Japanese sentiment in the United States ran rampant. Some Americans worried about national security and the threat Japan posed to the United States—especially on the West Coast. In February 1942, President Franklin D. Roosevelt signed Executive Order 9066, which allowed the government to incarcerate people of Japanese ancestry living in the United States. At the time, there were around 125,000 people of Japanese descent in the country. The majority of them were US citizens. Those who lived in California, Arizona, Oregon, and Washington were forced to move to relocation centers, taking only what they could carry. They had to quickly sell homes and businesses, abandoning what they could not sell. They were moved to incarceration camps, where they lived in hastily built shacks or at racetracks in converted horse stalls. In some camps, families lived in close quarters, but other times men were sent to one camp and their wives and children to another. In total, about 100,000 people were forced from their homes.

Late in World War II (1939–1945), some young Japanese Americans were allowed to leave the camps. Some went to universities to study. Young men were drafted or volunteered to join the military. Others served in military intelligence, helping make battlefield translations on the Pacific front.

There are many instances of racial violence in US history. People have worked to bring these issues to light, but racial violence has not been eliminated in the United States. Many people are victims of this violence, including Black people, Native Americans, and Asian people.

Massacres and Riots

The Chinese Massacre of 1871 took place on October 24 of that year in Los Angeles, California. Two Chinese gangs exchanged gunfire, and two police officers moved in to make an arrest. In the subsequent fight, one officer was injured and a civilian who was helping them was killed. In response, approximately 500 white and Hispanic rioters entered Chinatown. The rioters broke through the doors of a building where people were hiding. The rioters seized men and boys, beating, mutilating, and hanging them with rope or clothesline. Nineteen Chinese immigrants, including one teenager, were killed. Only one of them had been involved in the original incident. No one was convicted of the killings in the massacre.

A second event, the Rock Springs Riot, occurred on September 2, 1885, in Rock Springs, Wyoming. There was a conflict about which group of miners would work a rich coal deposit. A white mob killed twenty-eight and injured fifteen Chinese miners. There were no convictions. Additional attacks followed throughout the western United States.

CHAPTER TWO

Shootings of Black People

In 2021, there were 1,055 fatal police shootings in the United States. Black people made up 13 percent of the nation's population but 27 percent of those fatally shot by law enforcement. Police violence against Black people is not new. It's been happening since the police force was established in the 1800s.

In 2012, protesters in Florida sought justice for Trayvon Martin, a Black teenager who was shot and killed. The shootings of unarmed Black people continued to be an issue into the 2020s.

Not all shootings of Black people happen at the hands of police, however. On February 26, 2012, a neighborhood watch captain named George Zimmerman called 911. He reported that he saw a suspicious person walking in the rain in his neighborhood in Sanford, Florida. He was told to remain in his vehicle and not to approach the individual.

Zimmerman did not stay in his vehicle. Armed with a handgun, he got out and confronted the young man, seventeen-year-old Trayvon Martin. During the encounter, Zimmerman shot and killed Martin.

Zimmerman was charged with second-degree murder and manslaughter. During the trial, Zimmerman's defense lawyers released a video of Zimmerman reenacting the attack for the Sanford Police. He led them through the neighborhood to where the struggle took place and stated that Martin had him on the ground on his back. When Zimmerman said that Martin had grabbed his gun, Zimmerman reached behind his hip where he had carried his weapon. With this, Zimmerman was suggesting that Martin had seen the gun in the dark, in the rain, and while it was behind Zimmerman's back. On July 13, 2013, the jury found Zimmerman not guilty.

Black people and their supporters spoke out. Many were frustrated that Zimmerman had taken the law into his own hands. "This person did not have a badge," said documentary filmmaker Jenner Furst. "This person had not been trained in how to operate a firearm in the case of an emergency and not been trained in conflict management, had no skills for determining who is and who isn't the risk."[6]

> "This person did not have a badge. This person had not been trained in how to operate a firearm in the case of an emergency and not been trained in conflict management, had no skills for determining who is and who isn't the risk."
>
> —Jenner Furst, documentary filmmaker, discussing George Zimmerman and the killing of Trayvon Martin

Some people organized protests across the country. Others took to social media using the hashtag #BlackLivesMatter. As more and more people used the hashtag, momentum built and the movement grew.

The Impact of Police Brutality

Because it was a high-profile case and because of the growing Black Lives Matter movement, Martin's death helped many Americans become aware of the level of racial violence that

How Was Zimmerman Acquitted?

People wanted to know how George Zimmerman could be found not guilty of killing Trayvon Martin. After all, Martin was dead, and Zimmerman was the person who killed him. Legal analysts had a lot to say about this case.

The first issue was with the charges filed. The jury could have found Zimmerman guilty of either second-degree murder or manslaughter. A second-degree murder charge meant that Zimmerman acted out of hatred, ill will, or spite. Manslaughter meant he acted with an intent to do harm. It is very hard to know what a person is thinking. The second issue was with the evidence. Physical evidence might include DNA evidence under Martin's fingernails or on his clothing, but this type of evidence could have been washed away or affected by the night's rain. Most of the evidence in this case was testimony, including the testimony of Zimmerman himself. Rachel Jeantel was on the phone with Martin during the attack but only came forward reluctantly as a witness. She appeared combative and argumentative when she gave her testimony. Jeantel made a bad impression on the jury when she referred to Zimmerman as a "creepy-ass cracker" and referred to something as "retarded." Legal experts believed these factors led to an acquittal for Zimmerman.

Chelsea J. Carter and Holly Yan, "Why This Verdict? Five Things That Led to Zimmerman's Acquittal," CNN, July 15, 2013. www.cnn.com.

> "What we found was that every police shooting of an unarmed Black person was linked to worse mental health for the entire Black population in the state where that shooting had occurred."
> —Professor David R. Williams, chair of the Department of Social and Behavioral Science at Harvard University

Black people face in the United States. According to *Newsweek* magazine, Black people are killed three times as often by police as white people. These killings matter in terms of human lives lost. They also matter to the families of the victims, but it goes beyond that. A growing body of evidence shows that these killings take a toll on the Black community.

David R. Williams is the chair of the Department of Social and Behavioral Sciences at Harvard University. In 2018, he led a group of researchers in looking at how the killings of unarmed Black people by police impact the mental health of Black Americans. "What we sought to do was to identify if a police killing of civilians had negative effects not just on the victim's family, immediate relatives and friends, but on the larger community," said Williams.[7]

The findings surprised many people. "What we found was that every police shooting of an unarmed Black person was linked to worse mental health for the entire Black population in the state where that shooting had occurred," said Williams.[8] The information that Williams and his team gathered showed that the mental health impact lasted for three months following the death.

Williams and his team didn't stop at simply gathering data on mental health following a killing. They also looked at how everyday racism impacts mental health. "There are day-to-day indignities that chip away at the well-being of populations of color: How often do people act as if you are not smart? How often do people act as if they are afraid of you? We found what we call in scientific research a 'dose-response relationship' between the number of stressors individuals score high on and the number of depressive symptoms. So the more domains of stress you are high on, the higher are your levels of depressive symptoms. So reports of discrimination are linked to worse mental health," said Williams.[9]

Williams and his colleagues wanted to know if racial violence impacted other groups in terms of mental health. They found no measurable correlation between the deaths of unarmed Black people and the mental health of white Americans. There was also no measurable correlation between police killings of white Americans and the mental health of other white Americans.

With evidence that racial violence impacts mental health in Black communities, public health officials can develop ways to improve people's health. "Addressing this problem will require interventions to reduce the prevalence of police killings as well as programs that mitigate the adverse mental health effects in communities when these events occur," said Jacob Bor, who led the study with Williams. Bor emphasizes that structural racism can strongly impact mental health. Structural racism refers to the ways that a society reinforces racism through its laws and practices. For example, a court system that favors the police over Black shooting victims acts to reinforce racism and racial violence. Bor explains that tackling structural racism is essential. "Efforts to reduce health disparities should explicitly target structural racism," said Bor.[10]

The Court of Public Opinion

Black victims often suffer in the court of public opinion. For instance, before Zimmerman's case went to trial, stories about Martin appeared in the media. It came out that he had skipped school and been suspended for writing "WTF" on a locker. Another story detailed information from the forensics report, noting that he had THC, a chemical in marijuana, in his system.

The night Martin died, he was walking to his dad's home after visiting a convenience store. While members of the jury were being questioned during the selection process, one potential juror criticized Martin's parents. "Being a single parent with two boys of my own," they said, "I don't want to judge, but I just want to say this could have been prevented had he not been up here."[11]

The person was questioning whether Martin should have been walking through the neighborhood where he was shot and whether his parents were doing their job.

Something similar happened after George Floyd was murdered on May 25, 2020. That day, a store clerk in Minneapolis, Minnesota, called police, saying that Floyd made a purchase with a fake twenty-dollar bill. Police arrived and spotted Floyd sitting in a car. One officer drew his gun and demanded that Floyd get out of the car, pulling Floyd out of the vehicle. Floyd resisted but then cooperated once he was cuffed. When officers tried to put Floyd into their police car, he stiffened and fell to the ground, telling them he was claustrophobic and afraid of being confined.

Officer Derek Chauvin placed his knee on Floyd's neck and kept it there for more than nine minutes. Floyd repeatedly said that

Minimizing the Damage

Professor David R. Williams emphasized that there are things that people in the Black community can do to improve their mental health even in the face of racism. Williams stated that certain hormones can be found when someone is under stress, including stress from experiencing racism. But when teens had strong relationships with their families, teachers, and friends, these high hormonal levels were absent. "The quality of social ties seems to be an effective strategy to reduce all or at least some of the negative effects of discrimination. Building that sense of community is important," he said.

Williams described a study of teen suicide rates in Native communities in Canada. In communities that challenged the Canadian government for more rights, better health care, and control of their own communities, there were no suicides. "It suggests that being engaged and fighting for one's future and trying to make a difference is actually a resource that is protective for at least some mental health outcomes," said Williams.

Christina Pazzanese, "How Unjust Police Killings Damage the Mental Health of Black Americans," Harvard Gazette, May 13, 2021, https://news.harvard.edu.

he could not breathe and eventually stopped moving. Medical personnel arrived and brought Floyd to the hospital, but his heart had stopped and he was pronounced dead.

In the time before Chauvin's trial, it came out in the press that Floyd had been arrested in August 2007. He'd been charged with aggravated robbery after he and five other men entered a woman's apartment. Floyd pushed a pistol into her stomach while the others searched for things to steal. He was sentenced to five years in prison. In addition to this crime, newspapers repeatedly said he was resisting arrest when he died in 2020.

The coroner's report, a medical document that analyzed Floyd's condition at the time of his death, was also discussed in the media. The report showed that Floyd had a disease called COVID-19, which can lead to difficulty breathing. He also tested

George Floyd's murder sparked nationwide protests. At the height of the protests, approximately half a million people participated in almost 550 places.

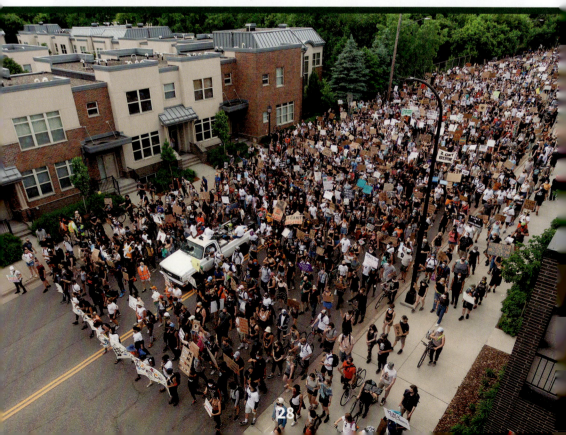

positive for two different drugs, fentanyl and meth. Despite these findings, the coroner did not say that they were the cause of death.

At Duke University, a bulletin board was assembled for Black History Month in February 2021. Someone made an addition to the display, hanging a printout of Floyd's toxicology report. On the printout, the person wrote: "Mix of drugs presents in difficulty breathing! Overdose? Good Man? Use of fake currency is a felony!"[12] This person wanted to criticize Floyd's character and absolve Chauvin of any guilt in Floyd's death.

No Evidence of Widespread Bias?

Heather Mac Donald works at the Manhattan Institute, a conservative think tank that focuses on domestic policy and urban affairs. She is also the author of *The War on Cops*, which was published in 2016. Mac Donald believes violent crime in the United States is on the rise because the police are under attack. She says there is no racism in policing. Mac Donald also says that demands for anti-racist reforms in the criminal justice system are putting lives at risk, because violent crime is on the rise. But data from the Bureau of Justice Statistics shows that before her book was published, the violent crime rate dropped from 26.1 incidents per 1,000 people in 2012 to just below 20 per 1,000 in 2015. Using FBI data, the Pew Research Center showed that between 1993 and 2019 the violent crime rate in the United States dropped 49 percent.

Writing about her book, author Tim Lynch pointed out that Mac Donald ignores certain facts. One is the reality that police treat Black and white people differently. Lynch was present at a bank robbery. The suspect, as seen by Lynch and others, was a Black male. Before Lynch left the area, the police had returned with two Black men, wanting to know if they had robbed the bank. Lynch explained that if the suspect was described as a white man, the police would not detain and bring in every white man they saw.

Matt Mohn was the student who found this printout on the bulletin board in his dormitory building. Although it was promptly removed, photos were taken and circulated among the students. Mohn was shocked that someone had gone to so much trouble to strip Floyd of his humanity. Mohn felt that this person had a message for all Black students: Floyd had deserved to die.

Mohn wasn't alone. Michael Manns, a Black student who lived down the hall from the board, said, "I was honestly terrified; I remember shaking in that moment. That happened right down the hall from where I sleep, from where I'm supposed to be safe. . . . The thought that it could be someone I've lived with all these months really terrified me."[13] Putting the printout on a Black History Month bulletin board felt like an open threat and a statement of who was a valuable human being and who was not.

University officials launched an investigation, announcing that if found the culprit would be punished. Manns said that the investigation helped him feel a little safer, but he also acknowledged that racism is not a new thing at the school. "They like to push this notion that at Duke, there's a bubble and racism can't get in," Manns said. "The reality is, it does happen and racism is allowed to grow here."[14]

Difficulties in Disciplining Officers

Racism and racial violence are hard to combat for a variety of reasons. For one, disciplining police officers in the United States can be difficult. Union contracts and bills of rights for law enforcement personnel clearly state the rights of police officers. These documents detail when an officer can be fired and what steps must be taken before this can happen. With these documents and procedures in place, police unions can sometimes block investigations and shield officers from discipline either by paying for lawyers or by encouraging politicians to pass laws that benefit police.

Police departments must look into the backgrounds of the officers they hire. In 2020, the *Yale Law Journal* published a study that examined the records of all police officers employed in Florida from 1988 to 2016. The study found that in any year,

In 2014, people waited to hear whether Officer Darren Wilson would be charged with Brown's death. A grand jury decided not to bring criminal charges against Wilson, leading to more protests.

3 percent of police working in Florida had previously been fired or resigned before being fired from their department for misconduct, including beating someone in the head and pistol-whipping a minor. Yet these officers had again found employment in other police forces.

Since 2014, efforts have increased to collect more complete data on the use of police force. This was the year when protests following the death of Michael Brown in Ferguson, Missouri, shocked the nation. On August 9, Brown and a friend were walking down the street when police officer Darren Wilson told them to walk on the sidewalk. They argued, then struggled, and Wilson shot and killed Brown.

One study was conducted by the University of Louisville and the University of South Carolina. It determined that in 2015, a Black man was 2.5 times more likely to be killed by a police officer than a white man. Black victims of police shootings are also less likely to be armed compared to white victims. Data collection and reporting is entirely voluntary on the part of agencies and officers. Information about police shootings is reported by only about 40 percent of all officers.

Lawrence Sherman is the director of the Cambridge Centre for Evidence-Based Policing. He says that US states should have the power to revoke a person's right to serve as an officer. "If a state agency was keeping track of everyone's disciplinary history, they might have taken Derek Chauvin out of the policing business ten years ago," says Sherman. Chauvin had received eighteen complaints against him before he killed Floyd. "We monitor performance of doctors," Sherman adds. "Why don't we monitor the performance of police officers?"[15]

Robin Engel is the director of the Center for Police Research and Policy in Cincinnati, Ohio. She says there is little knowledge about what works and what does not in terms of policing. "We're operating in the dark about what are the most effective strategies, tactics, and policies to move forward with," Engel says.[16]

Still, there have been some positive results from studies. For example, data shows that when officers cannot choose when to turn their body cameras off, wearing cameras corresponds with both fewer complaints and less use of force. Transparency may be part of the answer in reducing police violence against Black people in the United States.

> "We monitor performance of doctors. Why don't we monitor the performance of police officers?"
> —Lawrence Sherman, director of the Cambridge Centre for Evidence-Based Policing

Some people have called for police reform in the United States. They believe police officers are more aggressive than necessary when interacting with the public.

CHAPTER THREE

Violence Against Native Women

In June 2021, Gabby Petito and her fiancé Brian Laundrie started a cross-country road trip. They planned to visit state and national parks in the western United States and end the trip on the West Coast. Petito stayed in contact with her family until the end of August, when all communication stopped. Her family reported her missing, and the story flooded both social media and traditional media. Petito's

The first Indigenous Peoples March took place in 2019. It raised awareness for issues affecting Native peoples, including missing and murdered Native women and girls.

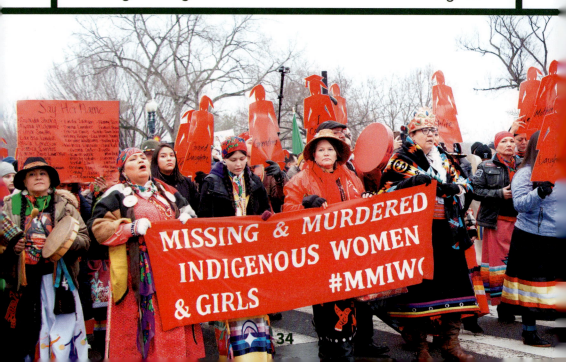

body was discovered on September 19, 2021, in the Bridger-Teton National Forest in Wyoming. She had been murdered.

Seeing Petito's story constantly highlighted in the news reminded many people how differently the cases of Native American and Alaskan Native women are handled. In a one-week period ending on September 22, 2021, Petito's story was mentioned 398 times on Fox News, 346 times on CNN, and one hundred times on MSNBC, according to a tally made by the *Washington Post*. This contrasted sharply with the case of Kiana Klomp.

Kiana was seventeen years old when she disappeared in 2019. She had run away from home in Post Falls, Idaho, but her mother, Teri Deschene, knew where she was staying with friends. Kiana

Where's the Attention?

"Where's the attention for ours? Where's the attention for Ruthie Fawn Kindness? . . . Rosalita Longee, where's her attention? She was a beautiful young Native woman, where's the FBI searches and the camera crew and the dog squad to find her?" said Carolyn DeFord, the founder of the Missing and Murdered Native Americans Facebook page. Ruthie Fawn Kindness disappeared in 2011 after calling her mother from a pay phone in Parkland, Washington. Rosalita Longee is a member of the Fort Peck Assiniboine and Sioux Tribes who went missing in 2015 from her grandmother's home in Wapato, Washington.

DeFord said that there should be some consistency in what families can expect from an investigation. At the very least, she says, law enforcement should provide a poster, the police report, and a list of resources including advocacy groups like Missing and Murdered Native Americans, missing persons databases, and media outlets to contact. They should not be left wondering where to turn and if anyone is looking for their daughters.

Hallie Golden, "Families of Missing and Murdered Native Women Ask: 'Where's the Attention for Ours?'" Guardian, September 24, 2021. www.theguardian.com.

later moved in with a man, but her mother still knew where she was until she disappeared.

Deschene, a member of the Tlingit Tribe, put up fliers and posted on social media. When she approached the traditional media, no one was interested in her daughter's story. "All I got in my pocket is Facebook, and just social media. That's all I got. I don't get any help from any other place. I begged. I just feel left out and unimportant," Deschene said.[17] Despite her efforts, not one story aired, and her situation is not unique. There is almost no media coverage when Native women go missing. In 2021, Kiana was found, but no stories aired about what had happened to her.

> "Violence towards people of color and women of color seems more routine. Women of color are often seen as being victims of their own mistakes."
> —Ignacio Garcia, professor of Western and Latino history at Brigham Young University

As Petito's case unfolded, journalist Joy Reid brought up the phenomenon that some people call "missing white woman syndrome." This refers to the unequal coverage that the media gives to white people versus people of color. "Why not the same media attention when people of color go missing?" asked Reid. "If the woman who is missing looks like your own daughter or granddaughter, and you're a newsroom executive, you're going to gravitate more toward it," she added.[18] Reid also noted that the racial makeup of newsroom executives is why women of color don't receive as much attention—they don't look like family. Racial and ethnic minorities were 40 percent of the US population in 2018 but made up only about 17 percent of newsroom staff, half of whom were white men.

Part of the problem is how society thinks of white women versus women of color. Ignacio Garcia is a professor of Western and Latino history at Brigham Young University. In 2021, he explained to reporters that white women are seen as helpless victims in the face of tragic violence. "Violence towards people of color and women of color seems more routine. Women of color are often seen as being victims of their own mistakes," Garcia said.[19]

The Numbers

In a 2016 study, the National Institute of Justice discovered that 84.3 percent of Native American and Alaskan Native women have experienced violence. This total includes 56.1 percent who are victims of sexual violence such as rape. Native men do not escape unscathed, and 81.6 percent of them have also experienced violence.

This violence can be fatal. According to the Centers for Disease Control and Prevention, murder is the third-leading cause of death

In June 2019, a memorial was set up for missing and murdered Native women in Oklahoma.

for Native women living on reservations. Their murder rate is ten times higher than that of women who do not live on a reservation.

Missing Women and Missing Data

It is hard to determine just how many Native women and girls are missing because not every case is reported as a missing person. Perhaps the best source of information is the National Crime Information Center (NCIC), a computerized index that records information on missing people and criminal information. Maintained by the FBI, it pulls together information from state, local, and federal law enforcement agencies. Data in the NCIC is accessible by law enforcement but not by the public. In 2016, the NCIC recorded 5,712 reports of missing Native women.

Another database is the National Missing and Unidentified Persons System, or NamUs. It is maintained by the US Department of Justice and is accessible by both law enforcement and the public. In 2016, only 116 cases of missing or unidentified Native women had been logged into the NamUs system.

The large disparity in the number of cases involving Native women that were recorded in NCIC and NamUs disturbed researchers from the Urban Indian Health Institute. Used by the public, law enforcement, medical examiners, and coroners, NamUs is a vital resource for spotting patterns in disappearances and spreading the word about missing people. The difference in the two tallies made these researchers realize that many cases

Misidentified

One problem in trying to quantify how many Native women are killed each year is the difficulty in identifying human remains. If someone is found without any identification, such as a driver's license or student ID, investigators write up a report and fill in as much identifying information as possible including height, weight, and approximate age. But when it comes time to make a racial identification, Native women may be identified as Hispanic or Asian. This mistake can make it even harder for their friends and family to find them.

involving Native women were falling through the cracks. Without the data on these missing person cases being readily accessible, they were less likely to be solved.

Criticism of NamUs followed the Urban Indian Health Institute's findings. Because of this, NamUs updated its database to include a field for tribal affiliation. This field would report a person's tribal status, whether he or she went missing from tribal land—such as a reservation—or an urban center. This information can help a family identify remains. It can also help law enforcement spot patterns.

Annita Lucchesi is a Montana-based researcher of Cheyenne descent. She specializes in cases involving missing Native people. She has used NamUs following the update and said that the new fields are not helpful because law enforcement personnel don't fill them in. "The cases that were already in NamUs, none of them have tribal affiliation listed. It's optional and law enforcement don't ask, so they don't put it in," she said.[20]

In her work preparing reports on missing persons, Lucchesi collected information on Sumi Gail Juan, a member of the Hoopa Valley Tribe who went missing in 2010. Lucchesi found that NamUs still lists Juan's tribal affiliation as "unknown." In October 2021, NamUs listed "unknown" as the tribal affiliation for 75 percent of the 748 cases of Native women and girls. Other frequent omissions include whether the woman went missing from tribal land or lived on tribal land. Missing information matters because more information means that law enforcement has a better chance of making connections that will solve a case. Researchers like Lucchesi seldom use NamUs because of the missing information. They instead turn to the Missing and Murdered Indigenous Women and Girls database created by the Sovereign Bodies Institute of which Lucchesi is the head. This group seeks to put Native people in charge of their own information instead of relying on government agencies.

Sex Trafficking

Sex trafficking is a serious crime that affects tens of thousands of people. It occurs anytime someone is recruited or forced to

Some public spaces have numbers people can call for help if they or someone they know is a victim of sex trafficking. Experts estimate that about 27.6 million people worldwide are victims of human trafficking.

have sex. This force can be physical violence, emotional coercion, or intimidation. People become victims of sex trafficking for a multitude of reasons. Some victims may be desperate for basic needs such as shelter and food. Others may have been in a relationship with the trafficker, who coerces them into doing sexual acts.

    Native people have high rates of being victims of sex trafficking. They make up approximately 1.1 percent of the US population but are nearly 25 percent of those who have been trafficked. Girls as young as thirteen years old are coerced into having sex for money or drugs or to prevent acts of violence against their families. Searchlight New Mexico is an independent news organization that spent sixteen months investigating human trafficking in the state. The organization discovered that Native American women and girls are the least recognized and least protected population in the state. They are often overlooked by medical personal, law enforcement, and others who could provide help.

A large issue is that health care and educational authorities who encounter these young women don't recognize the signs of sex trafficking. This was the case with a teenager that Searchlight New Mexico called Eva. Although Eva had been in trouble at school and been arrested, no one recognized that her behavior was typical of a girl who had been trafficked. Anxious and depressed, Eva often remained silent. She had little sense of time and was often reported missing by her grandmother. She was thin and looked malnourished, as if she had not been eating properly, and she often had bruises. None of the medical workers, educators, or law enforcement officers realized what this meant. "Nobody saw me," Eva said. "Not until the very end."[21]

> "Nobody saw me. Not until the very end."
> —Eva, a teen who was trafficked

In December 2016, Eva was arrested in Albuquerque, New Mexico, for stealing her grandmother's pickup truck. She entered the Butterfly Healing Center in Taos, New Mexico—a behavioral health treatment center specifically for Native American teens. Only there did she start to tell counselors what had happened to her.

Valaura Imus-Nahsonhoya is an expert on trafficked Native Americans. She learned most of what she knows by talking to people who had been trafficked. She learned that sex traffickers target women and girls they see as vulnerable. There are labor traffickers too. These people look for men, women, and children to work in the oil fields, in sweatshops, and as domestic help.

Imus-Nahsonhoya has learned that Native Americans are vulnerable for several reasons. One reason is due to poverty. In the United States, approximately 15 percent of the US population lives in poverty. Twenty-seven percent of Native Americans, however, are impoverished. People who live in poverty take chances that other people would not take to earn money to support their families.

Other factors that make children vulnerable to sex trafficking include experiencing violence at home and exposure to alcohol or drugs. Another factor is that law enforcement agencies on reservations are often small and must patrol large areas. With few people policing large areas, criminals can often avoid detection.

Investigations Flounder

When family members suspect a missing woman or girl has been trafficked or killed, they often get little help even when they stay in contact with law enforcement. Nicole Wagon is a member of the Northern Arapaho Tribe. Her oldest daughter, Jocelyn Watt, was found shot to death in her home in 2019. The murder was still unsolved in 2022. In 2020, Wagon reported her younger daughter, Jada, missing. Weeks later Jada's body was found in a field. Law enforcement reported that the cause of death was drugs and hypothermia. Wagon believes her daughter was murdered because questions about her disappearance have not been

Signs a Young Person Is Being Trafficked

There are various signs that a young person might have fallen prey to trafficking. The first thing people can look for is if the young person has new, expensive gifts like a cell phone or clothing. This is often part of the grooming process as the trafficker works to make the young person feel special and gain her trust. A new, older boyfriend can be a warning sign, again as part of the grooming process. Other signs may be if a girl starts skipping school, does not arrive places when expected, or has other absences she cannot explain. Among the biggest signs are behavioral changes with a person acting angry or withdrawn, sleeping significantly more, staying up all night, or not eating.

answered. But her daughters' cases and those of other Native American women and girls do not get media attention or many investigative hours from law enforcement.

Jurisdictional issues are often cited for lack of investigation. Part of the problem is that reservation or tribal police have little authority when it comes to white suspects. For instance, when Officer Jerome Lucero of the Zia Pueblo reservation police pulled over a non-Native driver who was under the influence of heroin, he did not have the authority to arrest the driver. All he could do was hold the driver until non-tribal law enforcement arrived. Tribal police are allowed only to question and detain non-Indigenous suspects on tribal land, and those suspects must be turned over to non-tribal authorities for prosecution.

When Searchlight New Mexico investigated human trafficking, its staff shared Eva's story with more than a dozen people including tribal police officers, tribal officials, and former clinicians from the Indian Health Service, an agency of the federal government. No one was surprised by Eva's story or that no investigation had taken place. "Tribal agencies are understaffed, underfunded and undertrained in this type of response," says Darren Soland, Ramah Navajo police chief. "Once someone who is being victimized goes from tribal to state land . . . and maybe comes back, it's hard to get the agencies to reach out and communicate with each."[22]

A case can involve tribal police, state police, and the FBI. The FBI is in part responsible for investigating serious crimes that take place on reservation land. The attorneys in charge of trying these cases are from the federal prosecutor's office. In 2017, federal prosecutors declined to try nearly half of the cases that took place on reservation lands. The District of New Mexico US attorney's office declined to prosecute 69 percent of cases that had taken place on reservation lands, according to data from the TRAC research center at Syracuse University.

Mary Kathryn Nagle is a Cherokee Nation lawyer and counsel to the National Indigenous Women's Resource Center. She believes that so few of these cases are prosecuted because they are not sufficiently investigated. "We're letting the FBI off the hook way too easily. And I wish more senators would call them to account for how few investigations go anywhere. They need to have an oversight hearing on why the FBI is abdicating its duties," said Nagle.[23] Because the FBI and other investigative and judicial branches fail to arrest and convict, violence against Native women continues with little justice for the victims.

Seeking Justice

Some politicians are working to help solve the issue of violence against Native women. On November 26, 2019, President Donald Trump signed Executive Order 13898 to create the Task Force on Missing and Murdered American Indian and Alaska Natives. This new task force was meant to address unsolved cases. However, the ability of the task force, commonly known as Operation Lady Justice, to accomplish its goals has been questioned. Deb Haaland is a member of the Laguna Pueblo. At the time Trump's task force was created, she was also a Democratic congressperson from New Mexico. She voiced her concerns. "This plan doesn't include the adequate amount of funding that Tribes have continuously asked for or the coordination at the local and tribal level where they know the issue best," she said.[24]

After becoming secretary of the interior in 2021, Haaland took the solution a step further. That April, she created the Missing and Murdered Unit (MMU) within the Bureau of Indian Affairs. She noted:

> Violence against Indigenous peoples is a crisis that has been underfunded for decades. Far too often, murders and missing persons cases in Indian country go unsolved and unaddressed, leaving families and communities devastated. The new MMU unit will provide the resources and leadership to prioritize these cases and coordinate resources to hold people accountable, keep our communities safe, and provide closure for families.[25]

The MMU was met with some criticism as it worked to establish its own jurisdictional rights. When Rose Yazzie's daughter Ranelle Rose Bennett disappeared in June 2021, Yazzie contacted the local Navajo Nation police. It took the police more than a week to

> "Violence against Indigenous peoples is a crisis that has been underfunded for decades. Far too often, murders and missing persons cases in Indian country go unsolved and unaddressed, leaving families and communities devastated."
> —Deb Haaland, US secretary of the interior

file a missing persons report. A month later, when MMU agents arrived at her home, Yazzie thought things would change. By October 2021, she still hadn't heard anything about her daughter's whereabouts or the investigation, and Yazzie contacted one of the MMU agents. The agent told her they were waiting for the Navajo Nation police. Yazzie contacted the Navajo Nation police and was told they were waiting on the MMU. No one had been working on the case for months.

Darlene Gomez is an attorney who represents the Bennetts and several other families with missing or murdered relatives. She said none of them have been helped by the MMU, even after she reached out to the organization. Gomez said her clients are upset and feel like the MMU is failing them. She adds that she does not blame the individual agents because they are working with no real jurisdiction. Lack of investigation and prosecution enables crimes against Native women to continue. Some people think it will take more than new legislation to reduce this violence.

CHAPTER FOUR

Anti-Asian Violence

A stereotype is a widely held, oversimplified view of a group of people. The stereotype that Asian Americans must deal with is that they are all highly successful, academic overachievers who have everything they need to succeed and thus are expected to rise to the highest levels at school, at work, and in life. Asian Americans are sometimes called a *model minority*—a term first used in 1966 by sociologist William Petersen. He explained that despite racial prejudice, discrimination, hate crimes, and more, Japanese Americans had achieved a high socioeconomic status, meaning they were well educated and had good jobs. He credited their

Stereotypes can affect people at a very young age. These stereotypes can be harmful.

success to hard work and cultural values that included discipline and a strong work ethic.

Ellen Wu is an associate professor of history at Indiana University. She explained that calling Japanese Americans a model minority was not a compliment. Repeatedly putting this stereotype forward, according to Wu, was an effort by US leaders to show how well democracy and equal opportunity worked. In the United States, according to the model minority myth, immigrants could overcome racism and succeed.

This myth makes overcoming adversity more difficult for Asian Americans. "In American culture, we perceive Asians

Combating the Model Minority Myth

Quincy Surasmith is Thai and Chinese American and almost flunked out of high school because his teachers couldn't understand why he wasn't motivated to succeed. His parents were getting divorced, and doing worksheets after school just wasn't a priority for him. He believes the model minority myth is harmful. "Sometimes I feel like we're taught to deal with injustice by grinning and bearing it and just trying to prove we belong more by doing extra service," said Surasmith.

Surasmith is now the host and producer of *Asian Americana*, a podcast about Asian American culture and history that is seldom taught in schools. He combats the model minority myth by giving these untold stories a voice. Some of the stories that interest Surasmith include Japanese Americans who demanded reparations, or compensation, for World War II incarceration and Filipino Americans who worked to organize farmworkers in the 1900s. "The reality is Asian Americans have always been part of this country contributing, doing that service for ourselves and for the country and for our communities," said Surasmith.

Jennifer Liu, "How the Model Minority Myth Holds Asian Americans Back at Work—and What Companies Should Do," CNBC, May 3, 2021. www.cnbc.com.

to be the model minority, right? They tend to do well academically and make money, or at least that's our perception. Oftentimes Asians in America are overlooked as targets of hate speech or hate crimes," said Richard Medina, an associate professor at the University of Utah.[26]

Part of the problem with the myth is that Americans often see Asian Americans as a single group. They don't consider that Asian Americans represent many different cultures from different countries. Because they think of Asian Americans as privileged, they forget that they might also be the targets of hatred and prejudice. But during the COVID-19 pandemic, Asian Americans faced an increase in racial violence.

COVID-19 is an infectious disease caused by the SARS-CoV-2 virus. It first appeared in the city of Wuhan, China, in December 2019. In early 2020, it rapidly spread around the world as scientists and medical researchers worked to discover effective treatments. On January 20, 2020, the Centers for Disease Control and Prevention confirmed the first US case in this global pandemic.

Abraar Karan is a doctor at the Brigham and Women's Hospital and Harvard Medical School. He explained that the global health community still behaves as if the United States and Europe are more capable than other regions. This kind of thinking led some people to believe that if the virus had appeared somewhere other than China it would not have become a pandemic because China did not act quickly enough to control it.

The Chinese government's response was problematic in some ways. The government silenced doctors and failed to warn the public for six days as the infection spread to 3,000 people.

> "In American culture, we perceive Asians to be the model minority, right? They tend to do well academically and make money, or at least that's our perception. Oftentimes Asians in America are overlooked as targets of hate speech or hate crimes."
>
> —Richard Medina, an associate professor at the University of Utah

But when the government announced shelter-in-place measures, these efforts proved effective. Karan explained that China, other Asian countries, and several countries in Africa more effectively controlled outbreaks than did Western countries early in the pandemic.

Some politicians, including President Trump, called SARS-CoV-2 the "Chinese virus" despite warnings from the World Health Organization that this type of stigmatizing language would

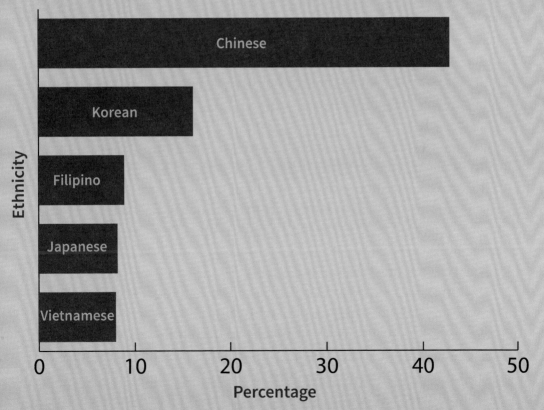

Asian Hate Crimes by Ethnicity

In 2021, Stop AAPI Hate reported the breakdown of Asian ethnicities that were most targeted for hate crimes in the United States.

Source: Aggie J. Yellow Horse et al., "Stop AAPI Hate National Report," *Stop AAPI Hate*, 2021. https://stopaapihate.org.

ultimately cast blame on Asians.²⁷ Elsa Marie D'Silva is an Aspen Institute New Voices fellow from India who studies violence and harassment. "What you're seeing in the U.S. is this pre-existing, deep-seated bias [against Asians and Asian Americans]—or rather, racism—that is now surfacing," says D'Silva. "COVID-19 is just an excuse."²⁸

Between the start of the pandemic and mid-2021, more than 9,000 incidents involving racism against Asians were reported in the United States. Some instances included actions that were not technically unlawful but were upsetting and frightening to victims nonetheless. Many attackers wrongly blamed Asian people for the ongoing pandemic. Some Asians were coughed on or refused service in restaurants and shops. Some people were spat on and verbally harassed. Others were told that they had the virus and needed to leave the country. Property was vandalized, and some people were attacked and killed.

Of the people harassed or attacked, 63 percent were women. Sometimes these incidents led to arrests. In December 2021, police in San Jose, California, arrested six men and charged them with at least 170 incidents that had taken place the previous year. The six men targeted more than one hundred Asian American women with robbery, burglary, and theft. Because these men so narrowly targeted their victims, they were also charged with hate crimes. Police praised the women for assisting in the investigation. "The community being willing to come forward and the courage of a victim to come forward and say, 'I'm not going to be a victim, I'm not going to let you do this to me' is absolutely critical. It was the purest example of collaboration," said San Jose Police Department captain Brian Shab.²⁹

Sometimes anti-Asian aggression takes a deadly turn. On March 16, 2021, Robert Aaron Long shot multiple people at three spas in Atlanta, Georgia. A total of eight people, including six Asian American women, died. Long explained that he targeted the spas for providing sexual temptation. He was charged with eight counts of murder. Although Long did not mention race, Sung Yeon Choimorrow noted that race cannot be ignored in this crime. Choimorrow is the executive director of the National Asian Pacific

Some Asian Americans have participated in anti-racism protests. In 2021, hate crimes against Asians were on the rise in the United States.

American Women's Forum. She explained that these women were targeted because of long-held stereotypes that hypersexualize Asian women, seeing them as promiscuous.

Robert Peterson, whose father is Black, was the son of one of the murdered women, Yong Ae Yue, who was Korean American. He said:

> We talked about her being targeted [for] being Asian, with this influx of hatred. Similarly [to] the way in which she talked about me, as a Black man, possibly being targeted if I engage with law enforcement. So, we both understood what it was like, but I guess we didn't let fear constrain our movement.[30]

He warns that violence against Asian Americans isn't going to be fixed by putting Long in jail or prosecuting any other single crime. Peterson believes that instead, people will have to be educated about racism by listening to each other's stories and by telling their own.

Steep Increase

It can be hard to know the true increase in anti-Asian hate crimes because many crimes go unreported. Denny Kim reported his attack only after he was encouraged to do so by a woman he met at a rally to raise awareness about anti-Asian hate crimes. Kim was attacked on February 16, 2021, in the Los Angeles neighborhood of Koreatown. Kim, a 27-year-old Korean American and US Air Force veteran, was waiting for a friend when two men ran up to him, yelling racial slurs and saying he had the Chinese virus and should go back to China. They hit him in the face, knocked him to the ground, and then began to kick and punch him. When Kim's friend arrived, the men ran away still yelling racist slurs. Despite his injuries, Kim didn't initially go to the police. "For a couple of days, I did not want to report this to the police because I remember those guys telling me that they're going to kill me," Kim said.[31]

Even with many unreported incidents, the data collected shows a steep increase in anti-Asian hate crimes. In the first half of

Many people have spoken out against anti-Asian hate crimes. However, instances of racism against Asians still occur.

2021, New York City had a surge of 395 percent in anti-Asian hate crimes compared to the previous year, as shown by crime statistics from the New York Police Department. The Asian-American-Pacific Islander (AAPI) Equity Alliance is a nonprofit organization that collects reports on hate crimes. It found that between March 2020 and September 2021, there was an incident increase of eleven times compared to the thirty years before the pandemic. When people reported incidents, they were asked to categorize what had taken place. They could select multiple types of discrimination because a single incident might include both verbal and physical components.

The largest single category, verbal harassment, made up 62.9 percent of the reported incidents. One incident detailed in the written report took place in Juneau, Alaska. The victim said, "I was accosted at the grocery store. A middle-aged man began yelling and blaming me for the 'Chinese Flu' and he told me to, 'Go home! Go back where you came from!'"[32]

Hate on Social Media

A 2022 study mapped anti-Asian hate speech on Twitter, starting with more than 4 million tweets that were sent between November 2019 and May 2020. The study looked for tweets that referred to COVID-19 and whether they were hateful. Hateful tweets used terms like *kung flu or Wuhan virus*. The researchers then mapped the point of origin of each hateful tweet. The strongest cluster, at a rate 300 times higher than the rest of the country, occurred in Ross County, Ohio. Other than this cluster, there were no identifiable patterns, and they were scattered evenly across the country. "The hope is that we can use hate in social media as a predictor of hate on the streets to use as an alarm for communities and public health officials to get the help and protection that they need," said associate professor Richard Medina, a coauthor of the study.

Michael Houck, "U of U Study Shows an Increase of Anti-Asian Hate Tweets After the COVID Pandemic," KSLTV, May 28, 2022, https://ksltv.com.

Other reported incidents include shunning or intentional avoidance, making up 16.3 percent. One Filipina woman who reported her experience to the AAPI Equity Alliance said that her family had been seated next to another family at an outdoor restaurant. A woman from the other family said that she didn't want to eat near the Asian family and that she had lost her appetite. She had her family's food boxed up then stormed out of the Columbia, South Carolina, restaurant.

Physical assaults made up 16.1 percent of the reported incidents. A student in Knoxville, Tennessee, was the victim of this kind of crime and said, "I was on my university campus and leaving one of my classes, which was held in a large auditorium-style room. I waited for most of the crowd to leave first. When I was in the doorway, a guy came up from behind, shoulder-checked me into the wall, and called me a 'Chinese b—' over his shoulder."[33]

The final 8.6 percent of reported incidents were online harassment. One student from Stillwater, Minnesota, said, "I had never experienced this type of racism towards me. A bunch of girls from my school messaged me saying, "Go back to China. Your eyes are weird and ugly. You don't belong here, c—."[34]

Social media and online communities are common places for harassment to take place because anonymity emboldens people to speak hate. But as shown in the AAPI Equity Alliance report, 31.2 percent of racist incidents against Asian people took place in public streets. A person in Brooklyn, New York, spoke about their experience: "A man standing on the sidewalk waited for me to pass in front of him. Then he spat a copious amount of saliva on the side of my head. He got on his bike and rode across the street. I walked after him, made eye contact, and asked why he did that. He yelled back at me, "F— you! F— you! Get out of my country."[35]

Another 26.8 percent of the incidents took place in public businesses such as restaurants. One incident was reported in Boston, Massachusetts: "I was the first one in line to pick up my order. The first thing the cashier said to me was, 'I don't speak Chinese,' and then they ignored me and served the next customer. After serving all the customers in line, they again said, 'I don't

> "As an Asian American female, I've seen that we can be targeted for what we look like. My friends started getting spit on and yelled slurs and being called, 'Chinese Virus.'"
>
> —Michelle Tran, a Chinese and Vietnamese American medical student

speak Chinese.' They walked away and waited for another person to serve me."[36]

Women were at higher risk for these negative encounters, with 62 percent of the incidents being reported by women. Michelle Tran is a medical student of Chinese and Vietnamese ancestry living in New York City. "As an Asian American female, I've seen that we can be targeted for what we look like. My friends started getting spit on and yelled slurs and being called, 'Chinese Virus,'" Tran said.[37]

Other racially motivated crimes against Asian Americans have been property crimes. One person reported that a racial slur had been carved into the top of their brother's car in Exeter, California. Restaurants owned by Asian Americans were also targeted in property crimes. The Jade Garden in Seattle, Washington, had its windows broken. In Yakima, Washington, Tony Yan, the owner of Minado Buffet, reported broken windows and graffiti spray-painted across the front of the building that read "take the corona [COVID-19] back."[38]

Taking Steps

People have taken various initiatives to reduce the number of anti-Asian hate crimes in the United States. On May 20, 2021, President Joe Biden signed the COVID-19 Hate Crimes Act to make reporting hate crimes easier. The bill works to simplify the reporting of hate crimes by assuring that online resources are available in multiple languages. Just before the bill was signed, Vice President Kamala Harris said, "This violence—it did not come from nowhere, and none of it is new. In my life, my lived experience, I have seen how hate can pervade our communities. I have seen how hate can impede our progress. And I have seen how people uniting against hate can strengthen our country. . . . Here's the truth: Racism exists in America. Xenophobia exists in America, antisemitism, Islamophobia, homophobia, transphobia—it all exists. And so the work to address injustice wherever it exists remains."[39]

The nonprofit organization Stop AAPI Hate pointed out that the legislation will not solve the problem. That's because it will not deal with most types of incidents that are reported to Stop AAPI Hate. Many of the reports the organization receives are about hateful but not illegal acts. For example, someone might tell a racist joke at work or in school. It is hateful and may be against policy, but it is not against the law.

One group that is working to help Asian Americans feel safe is Soar Over Hate. The organization was founded by Michelle Tran, Howard Chen, and Kenji Jones to combat xenophobia, or prejudice against people from other countries, and attacks on Asian American and Pacific Islander women. The group offers self-defense classes and has handed out more than 31,000 personal alarms, whistles, and cans of pepper spray in New York City and parts of California. A personal alarm can be activated to emit a loud siren. If threatened or attacked, the person carrying the alarm uses it to scare away their attacker and attract help.

In addition to classes and personal defense items, Soar Over Hate works to promote the well-being of the Asian American community. The group helps pay for therapy sessions for people who have experienced anti-Asian hate. It also provides scholarship money to high school students through its need-based Bright Futures Scholarship.

> "This violence—it did not come from nowhere, and none of it is new. In my life, my lived experience, I have seen how hate can pervade our communities. I have seen how hate can impede our progress. And I have seen how people uniting against hate can strengthen our country."
> —Vice President Kamala Harris

Racial violence has long been a part of life in the United States. It started as soon as settlers came into conflict with Native American peoples. It continued as enslaved people were forced to work and punished for seeking freedom. It impacted the lives of immigrants who were attacked for seeking work.

Racial violence continues today. As researchers collect data and study how these events impact individual people and society, they look for ways to break the patterns. One recommendation they have is to listen. By listening to the stories of people who have experienced racial violence, empathy will grow. With this comes the hope that the incidents of racial violence in the United States will decline.

In May 2021, the AAPI Care Fair took place in New York City. The event had information on housing rights and immigration, free health screenings, and self-defense classes.

SOURCE NOTES

Introduction: The Shooting of Stephon Clark

1. Quoted in Christina Carrega, "No Charges for Officers in Shooting Death of Unarmed Black Man, Stephon Clark: Sacramento District Attorney," *ABC News*, March 2, 2019. https://abcnews.go.com.

2. Quoted in Chris Hagan et al., "No Criminal Charges for Sacramento Police Officers Who Fatally Shot Stephon Clark," *NPR*, March 2, 2019. www.npr.org.

3. Quoted in Hagan et al., "No Criminal Charges for Sacramento Police Officers."

4. Quoted in Hagan et al., "No Criminal Charges for Sacramento Police Officers."

Chapter One: A Bloody History

5. Quoted in Kat Chow, "As Chinese Exclusion Act Turns 135, Experts Point to Parallels Today," *NPR*, May 5, 2017. www.npr.org.

Chapter Two: Shootings of Black People

6. Quoted in Deepti Hajela, "Trayvon Martin, 10 Years Later: Teen's Death Changes Nation," *AP News*, February 24, 2022. https://apnews.com.

7. Quoted in Christina Pazzanese, "How Unjust Police Killings Damage the Mental Health of Black Americans," *Harvard Gazette*, May 13, 2021. https://news.harvard.edu.

8. Quoted in Pazzanese, "How Unjust Police Killings Damage the Mental Health of Black Americans."

9. Quoted in Pazzanese, "How Unjust Police Killings Damage the Mental Health of Black Americans."

10. Quoted in Michelle Samuels, "Police Killings of Unarmed Black Men Affect Mental Health of Black Community," *BU Today*, June 25, 2018. www.bu.edu.

11. Quoted in Karen Grigsby Bates, "A Look Back at Trayvon Martin's Death, and the Movement It Inspired," *NPR*, July 31, 2018. www.npr.org.

12. Quoted in "A Printout of George Floyd's Toxicology Report Was Found on a Black History Display at Duke University, Insinuating That He Deserved to Die," *KESQ*, March 25, 2021. https://kesq.com.

13. Quoted in "A Printout of George Floyd's Toxicology Report."

14. Quoted in "A Printout of George Floyd's Toxicology Report."

15. Quoted in Lynne Peeples, "What the Data Say About Police Brutality and Racial Bias—and Which Reforms Might Work," *Nature*, June 19, 2020. www.nature.com.

16. Quoted in Peeples, "What the Data Say About Police Brutality and Racial Bias."

Chapter Three: Violence Against Native Women

17. Quoted in Hallie Golden, "Families of Missing and Murdered Native Women Ask: 'Where's the Attention for Ours?'" *Guardian*, September 24, 2021. www.theguardian.com.

18. Quoted in Jeremy Barr, "As the Gabby Petito Story Takes Over the News, Some Decry 'Missing White Woman Syndrome,'" *Washington Post*, September 24, 2021. www.washingtonpost.com.

19. Quoted in Melanie Andrews and Megan Spencer, "Gabby Petito Case Raises Media Ethics Issues About Coverage of Missing Persons," *Daily Universe*, November 18, 2021. https://universe.byu.edu.

20. Quoted in Braeden Waddell, "Incomplete Data Complicates the Search for Missing Native American Women," *US News*, November 21, 2021. www.usnews.com.

21. Quoted in Nick Pachelli, "'Nobody Saw Me:' Why Are So Many Native American Women and Girls Trafficked?" *Guardian*, December 18, 2019. www.theguardian.com.

22. Quoted in Pachelli, "Why Are So Many Native American Women and Girls Trafficked?"

23. Quoted in Pachelli, "Why Are So Many Native American Women and Girls Trafficked?"

24. Quoted in Sikowis (Christine Nobiss), "President Trump's Operation Lady Justice: The Truth About Violence to Native Women, Girls, LGBTQIA+," *Great Plains Action Society*, n.d. www.greatplainsaction.org.

25. Quoted in "Secretary Haaland Creates New Missing & Murdered Unit to Pursue Justice for Missing or Murdered American Indians and Alaskan Natives," *DOI*, April 1, 2021. www.doi.gov.

Chapter Four: Anti-Asian Violence

26. Quoted in Lisa Potter, "The 2020 Surge of Anti-Asian Hate Language," *University of Utah*, May 24, 2022. https://attheu.utah.edu.

27. Quoted in Laura Kurtzman, "Trump's 'Chinese Virus' Tweet Linked to Rise of Anti-Asian Hashtags on Twitter," *UCSF*, March 18, 2021. www.ucsf.edu.

28. Quoted in Joanne Lu, "Why Pandemics Give Birth to Hate: From Bubonic Plague to COVID-19," *NPR*, March 26, 2021. www.npr.org.

29. Quoted in Dustin Dorsey, "6 Men Charged with Hate Crimes After More Than 100 Asian Women Targeted in Bay Area Robberies," *ABC 7 News*, December 15, 2021. https://abc7news.com.

30. Quoted in Michelle Chen, "'She Could Have Been Your Mother:' Anti-Asian Racism a Year After the Atlanta Spa Shootings," *Guardian*, March 16, 2022. www.theguardian.com.

31. Quoted in Sarah Moon and Claire Colbert, "Attack on Asian American Man in LA's Koreatown Being Investigated as a Hate Crime," *CNN*, February 26, 2021. www.cnn.com.

32. Quoted in "Stop AAPI Hate National Report," *Stop AAPI Hate*, 2021. https://stopaapihate.org.

33. Quoted in "Stop AAPI Hate National Report."

34. Quoted in "Stop AAPI Hate National Report."

35. Quoted in "Stop AAPI Hate National Report."

36. Quoted in "Stop AAPI Hate National Report."

37. Quoted in Meg Dunn, "Horrified by the Surge of Anti-Asian Violence, She's Giving Her Community Tools to Protect Themselves," *CNN*, May 5, 2022. www.cnn.com.

38. Quoted in Sheng Peng, "Smashed Windows and Racist Graffiti: Vandals Target Asian Americans Amid Coronavirus," *NBC News*, April 19, 2020. www.nbcnews.com.

39. Quoted in Barbara Sprunt, "Here's What the New Hate Crimes Law Aims to Do as Attacks on Asian Americans Rise," *NPR*, May 20, 2021. www.npr.org.

FOR FURTHER RESEARCH

Books

Brandy Colbert, *Black Birds in the Sky: The Story and Legacy of the 1921 Tulsa Race Massacre*. New York: Harper Collins, 2021.

Sue Bradford Edwards, *What Are Race and Racism?* North Mankato, MN: Abdo, 2018.

Susan H. Kamei, *When Can We Go Back to America? Voices of Japanese American Incarceration During World War II*. New York: Simon and Schuster, 2021.

Internet Sources

Alice George, "Eighty Years After the US Incarcerated 120,000 Japanese Americans, Trauma and Scars Still Remain," *Smithsonian Magazine*, February 11, 2022. www.smithsonianmag.com.

Michael Houck, "U of U Study Shows an Increase of Anti-Asian Hate Tweets After the COVID Pandemic," *KSLTV*, May 28, 2022. https://ksltv.com.

Christina Pazzanese, "How Unjust Police Killings Damage the Mental Health of Black Americans," *Harvard Gazette*, May 13, 2021. https://news.harvard.edu.

Related Organizations

Black Lives Matter
https://blacklivesmatter.com
The Black Lives Matter website provides information on the movement and how people can get involved in protesting against racial violence.

Missing and Murdered Unit
www.bia.gov/service/mmu
The Missing and Murdered Unit's website provides information on the number of Native Americans who are affected by violence. It also explains the unit's role in investigating these crimes.

Stop AAPI Hate
https://stopaapihate.org
Stop AAPI Hate works to reduce hate incidents against Asian Americans and Pacific Islanders. The site has links to media articles and various reports published by the organization. The group also works to reduce systemic racism.

INDEX

American Civil War, 14–15
Apache Wars, 12
Asian Americana, 47
Asian-American-Pacific Islander (AAPI) Equity Alliance, 53–54

Biden, Joe, 55
Black Lives Matter, 24
body cameras, 32
Bor, Jacob, 26
Border Patrol, 19
Brown, Michael, 31

Centers for Disease Control and Prevention, 37, 48
Chauvin, Derek, 27–29, 32
Chinese Exclusion Act, 19–20
Chinese Massacre, 21
Choimorrow, Sung Yeon, 50–51
Clark, Stephon, 6–8
COVID-19, 28, 48–50, 53, 55
COVID-19 Hate Crimes Act, 55

Du Bois, W. E. B., 12

Engel, Robin, 32

Floyd, George, 27–30, 32

Garcia, Ignacio, 36–37

Haaland, Deb, 44–45
Harris, Kamala, 55–56
hate crimes, 9, 46, 48–50, 52–53, 55

incarceration camps, 20–21, 47
Indian Appropriations Act, 11
Indian Removal Act, 10–11

Juan, Sumi Gail, 39

Kim, Denny, 52
Klomp, Kiana, 35–36
Ku Klux Klan (KKK), 15, 19

Lee, Erika, 20
Long, Robert Aaron, 50–51
Lucchesi, Annita, 39
lynching, 8, 15, 17

Mac Donald, Heather, 29
Martin, Trayvon, 23–24, 26–27
Medina, Richard, 48, 53
Mexican-American War, 16
Missing and Murdered Indigenous Women and Girls database, 39
Missing and Murdered Unit (MMU), 44–45
missing white woman syndrome, 36
model minority, 46–48

NamUs, 38–39
National Asian Pacific American Women's Forum, 50–51
National Association for the Advancement of Colored People, 15
National Crime Information Center (NCIC), 38
National Indigenous Women's Resource Center, 43

Petito, Gabby, 34–36
police shootings, 6–9, 22–26, 31–32

Reid, Joy, 36
reservations, 11–12, 38–39, 42–43
riots, 15–16, 21
Roosevelt, Franklin D., 20

Schubert, Anne Marie, 7–8
Searchlight New Mexico, 40–41, 43
sex trafficking, 39–42
Sherman, Lawrence, 32
Sioux Wars, 12
Soar Over Hate, 56
social media, 24, 34, 36, 53–54
stereotype, 46–47, 51
Stop AAPI Hate, 49, 56

Task Force on Missing and Murdered American Indian and Alaska Natives, 44
Texas Rangers, 17–19
Till, Emmett, 15
Trail of Tears, 11
transatlantic slave trade, 13
Trump, Donald, 44, 49
Turner, Nat, 13–14

union contracts, 30
US Department of Justice, 9, 38

Watt, Jocelyn, 42
Williams, David R., 25–27
Wilson, Darren, 31
World War II, 21, 47
Wounded Knee Massacre, 13
Wu, Ellen, 47

Zimmerman, George, 23–24, 26

IMAGE CREDITS

Cover: © New Africa/Shutterstock Images
4 (top): © Picture History/Newscom
4 (bottom): © Everett Collection/Shutterstock Images
5 (top): © Ira Bostic/Shutterstock Images
5 (top middle): © Rich Pedroncelli/AP Images
5 (bottom middle): © Rena Schild/Shutterstock Images
5 (bottom): © Johnny Silvercloud/Shutterstock Images
7: © Rich Pedroncelli/AP Images
10: © Picture History/Newscom
11: © DCSHUTT/Shutterstock Images
14: © Everett Collection/Shutterstock Images
17: © Felix Marquez/AP Images
22: © Ira Bostic/Shutterstock Images
28: © Ben Hovland/Shutterstock Images
31: © a katz/Shutterstock Images
33: © Diego G Diaz/Shutterstock Images
34: © Rena Schild/Shutterstock Images
37: © Sue Ogrocki/AP Images
40: © Ted S. Warren/AP Images
46: © paulaphoto/Shutterstock Images
49: © Red Line Editorial
51: © Johnny Silvercloud/Shutterstock Images
52: © Sang Cheng/Shutterstock Images
57: © Steve Sanchez/Pacific Press Media Production Corp./Alamy Live News/Alamy
Back Cover: © New Africa/Shutterstock Images

ABOUT THE AUTHOR

Sue Bradford Edwards is a Missouri nonfiction author who writes about culture, social science topics, and history including race and women's history. She has written more than thirty books for young readers.